Front-Page News

adapted by Jodie Shepherd
adapted from the screenplay "Front Page News" by Scott Gray
illustrated by Carlo Lo Raso

Ready-to-Read

SIMON SPOTLIGHT/NICKELODEON
New York   London   Toronto   Sydney

Based on the TV series *Nick Jr. The Backyardigans*™ as seen on Nick Jr.®

SIMON SPOTLIGHT
An imprint of Simon & Schuster Children's Publishing Division
1230 Avenue of the Americas, New York, New York 10020
© 2010 Viacom International Inc. All rights reserved.
NICK JR., *Nick Jr. The Backyardigans*, and all related titles, logos, and characters are trademarks
of Viacom International Inc. NELVANA™ Nelvana Limited. CORUS™ Corus Entertainment Inc.
All rights reserved, including the right of reproduction in whole or in part in any form.
SIMON SPOTLIGHT, READY-TO-READ, and colophon
are registered trademarks of Simon & Schuster, Inc.
For information about special discounts for bulk purchases, please contact
Simon & Schuster Special Sales at 1-866-506-1949 or business@simonandschuster.com.
Manufactured in the United States of America, 0311 LAK
2 4 6 8 10 9 7 5 3
Library of Congress Cataloging-in-Publication Data
Shepherd, Jodie.
Front page news / adapted by Jodie Shepherd ; adapted from the episode "Front Page News"
by Scott Gray ; illustrated by Carlo Lo Raso. — 1st ed.
p. cm. — (Ready-to-read)
"Based on the TV series Nick Jr. The Backyardigans as seen on Nick Jr."—Copyright p.
ISBN 978-1-4169-8569-3
I. Gray, Scott. II. Lo Raso, Carlo. III. Backyardigans (Television program) IV. Title.
PZ7.S54373Fr 2010
[E]—dc22
2009023720

"**Snap!** I am .
TASHA

I take  for a ."
PICTURES   NEWSPAPER

 has another job, too.
TASHA

"But shhh! It is a secret.

Nobody knows but you!"

"I am Super Snap,

a superspeedy superhero."

 says.

TASHA

"I zip, zoom, spin, and snap.

I rescue those in need."

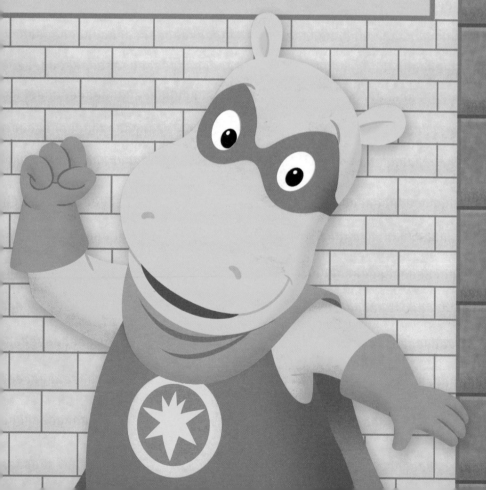

 's boss is  .

TASHA   PABLO

He runs the  .

NEWSPAPER

The  is called

NEWSPAPER

Bigopolis Big News.

"Say ' !'" says to .

CHEESE TASHA PABLO

"We have a problem, kid,"

answers .

PABLO

"There is no news and no PICTURE

for the front page!"

"I will get a for you,"

PICTURE

 says.

TASHA

"It has always been my dream

to take a front-page ."

PICTURE

The rings.

TELEPHONE

"A giant  is on Big Sea !'

ROBOT

BRIDGE

exclaims .

PABLO

"  is going to stop him?"

CAPTAIN BUBBLE

"Do not worry, boss," says .

TASHA

"I am on my way.

I will find **CAPTAIN BUBBLE** and

the .

ROBOT

I will take a in a snap!"

PICTURE

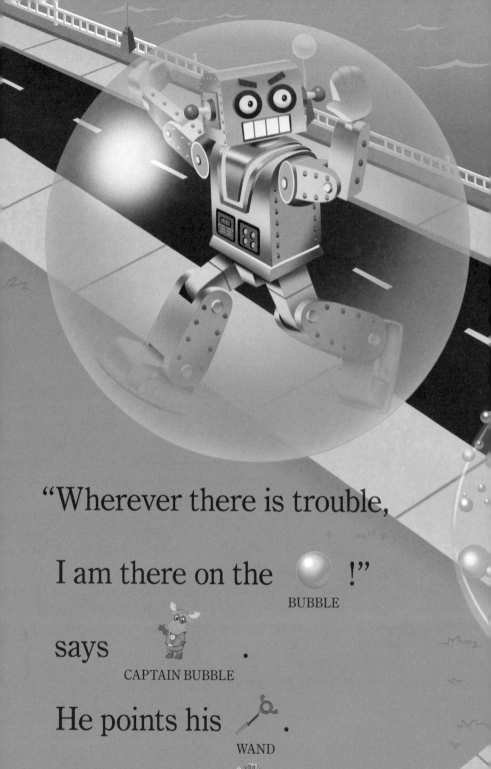

"Wherever there is trouble,

I am there on the !"
BUBBLE

says .
CAPTAIN BUBBLE

He points his .
WAND

He traps the inside a big
ROBOT   BUBBLE

"Say '  !'" says [TASHA].

CHEESE

The [BUBBLE] is running away.

The [ROBOT] is on the loose!

"Oh, no!" cries 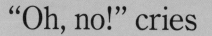 .

TASHA

" needs help!"

CAPTAIN BUBBLE

It is a job for Super Snap!"

 snaps. spins.

TASHA TASHA

 makes a !

TASHA TORNADO

The carries the away.

TORNADO   ROBOT

There is no for the .

PICTURE   NEWSPAPER

 will not be happy," says .

PABLO   TASHA

 is **not** happy.

PABLO

"Now we have no news.

The rings.

TELEPHONE

"Hello?" answers .

PABLO

"The is at the airport?

ROBOT

 will save the day?"

BUG GIRL

"And I will snap a ," says .

PICTURE   TASHA

The ROBOT is on the runway.

 BUG GIRL tries to lift the ROBOT

off of the runway.

Whoa! It is hard work.

 needs help fast.

BUG GIRL

Super Snap to the rescue!

The takes off into the .

ROBOT

CLOUDS

Still there is no .
PICTURE

 is **really** not happy.
PABLO

"We will never get a now!"
PICTURE

The rings.
TELEPHONE

"Look behind me?" asks .
PABLO

Through the he sees the !
WINDOW   ROBOT

And !
CAPTAIN BUBBLE

And !
BUG GIRL

 buzzes around the

BUG GIRL ROBOT

while makes

CAPTAIN BUBBLE

a wall.

BUBBLE

They stop the !

ROBOT

'Say '  !'" says .
CHEESE   TASHA

Crash! The is so excited,
ROBOT

he breaks the wall.
BUBBLE

 are everywhere!
BUBBLES

", , ," cries the

CHEESE CHEESE CHEESE ROBOT

 says, "The doesn't

TASHA ROBOT

want to **eat** .

CHEESE

The wants to **say** ' '."

ROBOT CHEESE

So uses her timer. **Snap!**

TASHA

"Great !" says .

PICTURE PABLO

"You saved my !

NEWSPAPER

"You saved the town, too!"

There is one more thing to do.

It is superhero snack time.

" !" everyone shouts.
CHEESE